This Is the Bird

George Shannon • *Illustrated by* David Soman

Houghton Mifflin Company
Boston 1997

To my prairie-born mother, Doris Irene
— G. S.

For Marvin and Barbara
— D. S.

For information about this and other Houghton Mifflin trade and reference books and multimedia products, visit The Bookstore at Houghton Mifflin on the World Wide Web at http://www.hmco.com/trade/.

Manufactured in the United States of America
HOR 10 9 8 7 6 5 4 3 2 1

The text of this book is set in 18 pt. Sabon Bold.
The illustrations are oil paint, reproduced in full color.

Library of Congress Cataloging-in-Publication Data
Shannon, George.
This is the bird / by George Shannon; illustrated by David Soman.
p. cm.
Summary: A cumulative tale about a wooden bird carved by a little girl's maternal ancestor, and passed down lovingly from mother to daughter through the generations.
ISBN 0-395-72037-0
[1. Mothers and daughters — Fiction.] I. Soman, David, ill. II. Title.
PZ7.S5287Th 1997
94-28974 CIP AC

This is the bird my great-great-great-great-great-grand-mother carved from a spoke while waiting for her baby in a small sod house, and didn't have a single tree to see.

This is the bird my great-great-great-great-grandmother hid — along with her ring — in the butter she was churning when the robbers came.

The bird *her* mother carved from a spoke while waiting for her baby in a small sod house, and didn't have a single tree to see.

This is the bird my great-great-great-grandmother, who couldn't hear a sound, sewed in her hem when she went away to school to learn to talk with her hands.

The bird *her* mother hid from the thieves.

The bird *her* mother carved from a spoke while waiting for her baby in a small sod house, and didn't have a single tree to see.

PUBLIC
POOL

This is the bird my great-great-grandmother grabbed as
she ran to the cellar when she was twelve and a tornado

The bird *her* mother sewed in her hem.

The bird *her* mother hid from the thieves.

The bird *her* mother carved from a spoke while waiting for her baby in a small sod house, and didn't have a single tree to see.

This is the bird my great-grandmother rubbed for luck when she told her father she didn't want the job he got her at the bank. She was going to go to college like she'd always dreamed.

The bird *her* mother saved in the storm.
The bird *her* mother sewed in her hem.
The bird *her* mother hid from the thieves.
The bird *her* mother carved from a spoke
while waiting for her baby in a small sod house,
and didn't have a single tree to see.

This is the bird my grandmother lost for years and felt so sad she filled the house with small wooden birds. Then found it again in the furnace vent and gave the rest away

The bird *her* mother rubbed for luck.
The bird *her* mother saved in the storm.
The bird *her* mother sewed in her hem.
The bird *her* mother hid from the thieves.
The bird *her* mother carved from a spoke while waiting for her baby in a small sod house, and didn't have a single tree to see.

This is the bird my mother unpacked first thing when she moved to the Arctic to teach first grade, and met my dad at the same little school.

The bird *her* mother found down the vent.
The bird *her* mother rubbed for luck.
The bird *her* mother saved in the storm.
The bird *her* mother sewed in her hem.
The bird *her* mother hid from the thieves.
The bird *her* mother carved from a spoke while waiting for her baby in a small sod house, and didn't have a single tree to see.

This is the bird my mother just gave *me* to celebrate trying again after falling last week on my first high dive and being too scared to ever dive again.

This is the bird I'll always keep till the right time comes to pass it along. The bird I got to celebrate my high dive.

The bird my mother unpacked first thing.

The bird *her* mother found down the vent.

The bird *her* mother rubbed for luck.

The bird *her* mother saved in the storm.

The bird *her* mother sewed in her hem.

The bird *her* mother hid from the thieves.

The bird *her* mother carved from a spoke while waiting for her baby in a small sod house, and didn't have a single tree to see.